THE

MYSTERIOUS

MELODY

Written by
SP K-Mushambi

Illustrated by
Kudzai Gumbo

Copyright ©2019: SP K-Mushambi

Published by Naniso Create
in association with Conscious Dreams Publishing
www.nanisocreate.com
Naniso Media Ltd
27 Old Gloucester Street
London, United Kingdom WC1N 3AX

Illustrated by Kudzai Gumbo

Edited by Rhoda Molife
www.molahmedia.com

Typeset by Oksana Kosovan

The moral rights of the author and illustrator have been asserted.

ISBN: 978-1-9161217-0-6

First printed in the United Kingdom 2019

For my beautiful daughters Danai & Tayana

To my mother Unity F Kandawasvika –
love always

Thank you. *Ndinotenda. Siyabonga.*

Firstly, to my husband Rutendo for your patience and invaluable support throughout my career and when pursuing new dreams. Thank you for being my sounding board, going through early drafts of this book and keeping the girls at bay while I was writing.

I am indebted to Kudzai Gumbo whose illustrations magically brought the characters that lived in my head to life. It has been inspiring to work with you.

A very special thank you to Rhoda Molife for your editorial help, insightful feedback and the time spent polishing this manuscript. Because of your effort and encouragement, a dream has turned into reality.

To Daniella Blechner and the team at Conscious Dream Publishing, I am thankful, inspired and humbled by your advice and commitment to my success. *Siyabonga.*

Rumbi Kawadza and Tapiwa Katiyo, I couldn't have done this without you. Your dedication, passion and time invested on this project from the start renewed my love for writing and creativity. *Ndinotenda.*

This book would not have been possible without the tremendous and unwavering support and enthusiasm from my family and friends. I am grateful to you all.

Thank you to my daughters Danai and Tayana – you inspire me daily not to give up and step out of comfort zones. You have cheered me on with your dancing, hugs, kisses, cups of tea and homemade coolers in frosty weather. I love you girls!

CONTENTS

CHAPTER 1

5 AM

Not again!

Naniso reluctantly opened her drowsy, brown eyes. She sighed, looked up at the ceiling then slowly gazed around her room. It was still dark except for the glow of the corridor light that crept in under the bedroom door.

The wardrobe was a monstrous silhouette and she could just about see the outline of the painting of an African village on the bedroom wall. That painting was one of *Amai's* most cherished possessions. Naniso remembered how special she felt the day her mother had hung it up in her room. She felt *Amai* had trusted that it would be safe there. On the other hand, Shinga, her twin, would probably not have been so careful with it, especially as his bedroom wall was covered in cheap posters of football and basketball players.

Naniso glanced at the clock on her bedside table. Not that she needed to check the time. Of course, it was five o'clock in the morning. Yes indeed, the same time she had been woken up on Monday, Tuesday, Wednesday and now Thursday. That was four mornings of broken sleep.

Something was not right.

'This is so annoying,' she thought to herself, idly tugging at her corn-rowed braids.

She realised her headwrap had come loose and so she tied it up again. Who wanted to be up so early when it was wintry cold and dark outside?

There were no birds chirping a morning song before the sound of planes took over the skies. It was even too early for Cooper, the dog from next door, to set off for his morning walk.

Naniso continued to lie still in bed, listening to the mysterious melody that had become her wake-up call. She had no idea where it was coming from. It wasn't *Amai's* phone alarm. That rang at six o'clock on the dot, Monday to Friday. It wasn't *Baba's* clock radio. When her father's alarm went off, it was loud enough to wake even the neighbours! Surprise, surprise it never woke *Baba* up.

The music floated through the family's terraced home. It had happy, rich and soothing tones. Beautiful as it was, it didn't change the fact that it had now disturbed her sleep four mornings in a row. She felt she'd heard it before, but where she couldn't recall. That added to the frustration of it all.

Naniso buried her head under the pillow. Maybe it was just her imagination. After all, no one else in the family seemed disturbed by the strange goings on. Soon though, the soothing melody made her drift back to sleep...

Shinga hunched over his sister. He wasn't sure how to wake her up. To be more specific, he wasn't sure which of his many mischievous methods he'd use to wake her up today. He thought of drawing a moustache on her face but that wouldn't be as funny as it was the first time. His sister was in the deepest of sleeps – not only was she snoring, she was drooling too. It was not a pretty sight. Oh, how he wished he had his phone with him. One picture of her and he would have been able to get back at his twin for all the times she'd pranked him. He saw a glass of water on her bedside table and smiled. This was going to be good! He dipped his fingers into the water and flicked cold droplets onto Naniso's face.

'Huh?!' Naniso woke with a start.

'You're late. What's going on?' asked Shinga before his sister had the chance to complain. He was already dressed in his school uniform with

his hair neatly brushed. Even his glasses were sparkling which was a surprise because he nearly always forgot to clean them.

'We're supposed to be leaving for school in fifteen minutes. If you're late, *Amai* won't take us to the park after school. I really want to ask the old lady you sit next to on that bench if she plays football. Golden Striker, that's what I've decided to call her.'

'I'm so tired Shinga. What are you on about? What old lady?' asked Naniso wearily, wiping her wet face. She was totally unamused.

Shinga noticed the scowl on his sister's face. Naniso was normally the first one up and annoyingly perky at that too. Today she had an important rehearsal at school, so she should have been up even earlier and should have been even more annoyingly perky. Instead, she looked so not ready to get out of bed. Suddenly, he regretted waking her the way he had.

'You better hurry up. *Baba* and *Amai* have been calling you for ages. They're getting impatient.'

Right on cue, *Baba's* voice boomed up the stairs.

'Naniso! *Kurumidza!*'

'You heard him. You better hurry,' Shinga urged his twin.

'There's this music that keeps waking me up,' Naniso continued as she got out of bed. 'It's been every day this week and now I'm really fed up. I wish it would stop,' she whined, sluggishly walking to the bathroom to get ready.

'You hear this weird music too?!' Shinga, asked his sister. 'I thought it was all in my head!'

Naniso stopped in her tracks.

'No joke?! Why didn't you say something?!' they both shouted in unison.

CHAPTER 2

IN THE PARK

School was done and Shinga wanted to go to the park. Naniso didn't, but *Amai* insisted. The excitement she'd felt after realizing that both her and her brother had been hearing the same music floating through their house each morning had long gone. Her day at school had been so miserable that she just wanted to go home. However, she was outnumbered. She dragged her feet to the park mumbling along the way.

19

In her left hand was her violin which felt extra heavy under the weight of her gloom. None of her friends were going to the park which only added to her misery. *Amai* kept pointing out that she was ruining her new shoes.

'We don't have a tree that grows money in our garden. *Famba zvakanaka*. Pick your feet up.'

'Duh,' Naniso muttered under her breath. 'Everyone knows money doesn't grow on trees.' Of course, she knew better than to say that out loud. But that didn't stop her from rolling her eyes and continuing with her slow plod.

The park was at its busiest because for once, it wasn't raining. It often rained after school. Sometimes it rained before school too. Other days it rained before **and** after school. It was safe to say that it rained a lot in England. Today though, the sky was blue despite the winter chill. Snug in her red coat Naniso found her favourite spot under the great oak tree. She dumped her violin case and school bag against the tree trunk and sat down.

On any other occasion, she would have watched the younger children either going 'round and 'round on the merry-go-round or flying high on the swings. Or, she would have been reading a book. Today she didn't feel like doing much because she was sad.

You see, Naniso was supposed to sing a solo for parents' assembly at the end of term. Now that's a splendid thing to do, wouldn't you say? Everything had been going so well in rehearsals earlier that morning until she croaked! That's right! She croaked so loud that even she was convinced there was a toad in the room. It was such a dreadful sound that had all but cancelled out their hard work getting the songs right. The whole class had laughed and sniggered. To make matters worse, Rita had stepped forward and rudely asked Miss Harrison, their music teacher, to take Naniso's part. Who does that?

'...and this is why I should have the lead Miss Harrison. I go to the School for Stars and I always get the main role. That's because I never make such terrible mistakes,' Rita had said.

Naniso had willed the ground to swallow her but it hadn't, and that was the start of her very bad day at school.

Now as she sat sadly under the oak tree, she decided she wouldn't go to school tomorrow. She had to find a way to stay at home. A headache maybe? No. *Amai* would easily fix that with a painkiller and a kiss. It needed to be something quite bad. Something...contagious! That's it! She would pretend she'd caught a stomach bug. No parent ever sent a child to school with a contagious illness like a stomach bug. In fact, parents and teachers always panicked when there was one going around. She pulled at her hair and then dramatically patted her afro puff neatly back in place, a gesture that meant the decision was final.

'OUCH!' Naniso suddenly cried out. Something rudely woke her from her daydreaming. 'Ouch! Ouch! Stop it!'

'Then get off my foot,' replied the voice of an old woman.

Naniso turned to her left to see a very old lady who had appeared from nowhere. Her huge emerald green earrings made her head look tiny. She poked Naniso several times with a weird-looking walking stick. The golden bangles on her wrists jingle-jangled as she did so. Naniso quickly moved away from the lady.

'I'm sorry. I didn't even know I was err...sitting on your foot,' she apologised, even though she was sure she'd been nowhere near this woman.

'No, of course you didn't,' replied the old lady. Then she cheerily asked, 'Cup of tea?'

Naniso's eyes widened. She could have sworn her new acquaintance had done a little dance complete with a leap in the air! She twisted her hair again as she tried to make sense of the woman before her who wore a gold and green African-print dress with matching headwrap. Her eyes looked sad, yet they twinkled at the corners. Naniso now noticed that her weird-looking walking stick was covered in a pattern that changed colours every few seconds. As she came to her senses, Naniso remembered that she wasn't supposed to be talking to strangers! Where was her bag, violin and Shinga anyway?

'Oh no! I've lost track of time. Where's *Amai*?' She swiftly picked up her school bag.

'It's ok,' said the old lady, sensing that Naniso was getting worried. 'All is fine...is fine. Look see.'

Naniso followed the direction of the old lady's long, wobbly index finger on which was a ring with a large, yellow stone. There was Shinga, ferociously playing football with his best friend Sanjay and their classmates. *Amai* was sitting on a park bench, deep in conversation with Sanjay's mum. Just then the old lady started shouting at her.

'Who are you?! What do you want?! Who are you?!' she shrieked, seemingly confused.

Naniso looked at her suspiciously. Had she really had a conversation with this woman or had it all been a figment of her imagination? Her mood had changed faster than when Shinga flipped from one TV channel to the next! As strange and weird and fascinating as this old lady with the gold and green African-print dress and large, green earrings was, Naniso decided it was time to join her mother and brother.

25

CHAPTER 3

GOLDEN STRIKER
IS GOGO ZANA

Naniso half-ran and half-walked to her mother. She heard heavy panting beside her. Surely it was not the old and obviously eccentric woman chasing her?

'Why are we running?'

It was Shinga. She was relieved to see him.

'From that weird old woman!' She gasped and stopped to catch her breath.

'From Golden Striker?' Shinga asked, surprised. 'Who?'

'I told you about her this morning, remember? The old lady who always sits under the oak tree. She always kindly kicks the football back to us whenever it rolls over to her. I bet she used to be a footballer when she was young. These old people are full of surprises you know?'

'C'mon now Shinga. That's ridiculous! Besides, I always sit under that tree when we come to the park and I've never seen her before.'

'You and Golden Striker sit under that tree together all the time Naniso. You sit on one side of the trunk and she sits on the other.'

Shinga looked at his sister's puzzled face. He was pleased that for once he knew something she didn't and to top it off, it was her business to know too!

Before Naniso could find something witty to say, Shinga ran back to his friends shouting, 'GOOAAALLLL!'

Sanjay had scored and Shinga just had to join in the celebration dance.

'Wowzer,' Naniso said to herself. Just then, she realised she'd left her violin under the oak tree. Half-heartedly, she turned back to get it. If what her brother had said was true, then Golden Striker, or whatever her name was, would be harmless. Maybe she lived in the old people's home across the road.

'Hello *muzukuru*,' Golden Striker greeted Naniso warmly, this time with a toothless grin. Naniso's heart melted because *muzukuru* is what her grandparents, *Sekuru* and *Mbuya* called her. It meant grandchild. She chuckled when she remembered that she too had adult grandchildren, and she was only ten. Anyway, that was a story for another time.

'Ah! You forgot your instrument,' Golden Striker pointed out before asking, again, 'Cup of tea?'

Her bangles jangled a rhythm as she signalled Naniso to sit next to her at a neatly laid table. Naniso stared in wonder. Where had the table with its tablecloth, teapot and teacups come from?

'I like tea. It helps me think. Sit. Sit please.'

Naniso cautiously sat down. She was curious to learn more about this odd woman who was not quite like anyone she'd ever met. Well, at least she could find out for Shinga if she played football. Before she settled down, she turned to look for *Amai* and checked in by waving vigorously. *Amai* waved back and signalled that they had ten minutes left to play. Naniso turned to look at Golden Striker who was waiting for an answer.

'Cup of tea?' she asked yet again, ready to pour the contents of the teapot in the cups in front of her.

'No thank you,' was Naniso's reply.

'Suit yourself,' Golden Striker said as she poured herself a cup, gently put the teapot down then took a sip – well more like a slurp – from the dainty cup.

They sat in silence, observing each other. Naniso wondered how old Golden Striker was. Her sad but twinkling eyes were a contrast to the many wrinkles on her face. The chunky, golden beaded necklace she wore seemed too heavy for her neck. There was an air of sophistication about

her though. Naniso suddenly remembered that it was rude to stare and turned to look at a bird searching for worms on the ground. It was then that she spotted a *mbira* resting against the tree. Her eyes lit up at the sight of the musical instrument. Even though *Amai* had a *mbira*, it wasn't every day that you saw one.

'I am Zana. *Gogo* Zana. Do you want to play something?' offered Golden Striker when she saw Naniso looking at the instrument. She picked it up and shooed the bird. 'Away with you *shiri*. You're supposed to be up there not down here,' she said sucking her gums in disappointment. The bird simply hopped away. *Gogo* Zana then handed the *mbira* to Naniso.

'Oh! Is that your name? *Gogo* Zana? My name is Naniso, but I only play the violin, piano and recorder. I don't play the *mbira*.' Naniso didn't want to seem clueless, so she added, 'We have a *mbira* at home though. It's in a box somewhere. My Mum wants to put it on the bookshelf as decoration.'

'*Ehee,*' *Gogo* Zana nodded thoughtfully. 'Well just try,' she urged.

Encouraged, Naniso's hands rested on the metal keys. They were shiny, and the *calabash* was smooth with colourful, swirly patterns painted all over it. Before she knew it, her thumbs started dancing over the keys, playing a somewhat familiar tune. To add to Naniso's surprise, *Gogo* Zana hummed along with her eyes closed as if she knew the song well. Copying *Gogo* Zana, she closed one eye, then the other. It felt just right.

Naniso's mind drifted back to the day's events, remembering her plan to bunk off school. She was not going to sing the solo. That was a fact as there was nothing worse than people laughing at you. Suddenly she stopped playing the *mbira*, and in a flash, handed it back to *Gogo* Zana. Gathering her things, she mumbled a hasty thank you and ran to her mother.

CHAPTER 4

THE INVESTIGATION

Friday morning just after five o'clock, Shinga quickly got out of bed, put on his glasses and dashed out of his bedroom. After trying to ignore the strange music, he'd had enough. It was time to put an end to the mystery. His bet was on one of Naniso's old, annoying toys that still had its batteries. As he reached the top of the stairs, he was joined by his sister who had tiptoed out of her bedroom into the hallway.

'What are you doing?' she whispered.

'I think the music is coming from under the stairs. I'm going to ask *Amai* and *Baba* for help because I'm fed up of waking up so early.'

'No! I'll help. Just don't wake them up.'

Naniso was curious to find out what the melody was too but she did not want her parents to interfere with her plans to skip school.

'What do you care anyway?' Shinga suddenly changed the subject. 'I know you faked being ill at dinner last night so that you don't have to go to school today. You should stay in bed remember.' He knew all the tricks to bunk off school because he'd tried practically all of them.

'I wish I was like Rita. She never messes things up,' Naniso tried to explain.

'Errr, no, you don't want to be like Rita,' he snapped back. 'She can be a bully at times.'

'You wouldn't understand,' she sighed.

'Just be you Naniso. That's all there is to it. Now, let's go, seeing as you're here to help me.'

Naniso glared at her brother but she knew she was defeated...this time.

They both gripped on to the banister and tiptoed down the stairs counting each step. They carefully stepped over the ninth and the eleventh which always creaked, no matter how many times *Baba* fixed them. Step twelve and they were downstairs.

The twins followed the music. As it got louder, they tightly clutched each other's hand. It seemed like ages before they were standing in front of the understairs cupboard. The mysterious melody was most certainly coming from there. Shinga flicked the corridor light switch on. Naniso quickly signalled him to turn it off. No way were their parents going to find her out of bed doing detective work. As soon as they found out what was going on, she was heading straight back to her room with her tummy bug. She would just have to make sure Shinga didn't snitch.

Naniso reached for the door handle. Suddenly there was silence. The music had stopped. They both stepped back from the door. This was like something out of a movie, but instead of being scared, they were now more curious than ever. What was going on?! They looked at each other searching for answers before making a silent agreement with a high five and linking their fingers.

'*Pamwe*!' they both whispered boldly.

This was their code to say they would have each other's back. With a nod, Shinga signalled Naniso to open the cupboard. In turn, she turned the handle and pushed the door open. It creaked loudly.

'Shhh...,' shushed Shinga, even louder than the door had creaked.

'I can't help it!' Naniso half-hissed and half-whispered back.

The cupboard was empty except for an old, flimsy cardboard box in the far right-hand corner. The twins could see it contained some of *Amai's* cherished possessions. They crept in, knelt beside the box and started rummaging.

'Be careful. *Amai* will be upset if we break anything,' said Naniso.

The old box contained several instruments: a *vuvuzela*, a *hosho*, a *ngoma* and a *mbira*.

The long kudu horn-shaped instrument *Baba* had brought back from the World Cup in South Africa excited Shinga and gave him an idea. He was just about to test the *vuvuzela* when steps nine and eleven gave the alarm that someone was coming down the stairs. They put the instruments back in the box as carefully and quietly as they could.

'What are you looking for?'

It was *Amai*. She was standing in the doorway. The twins gulped. They were busted! How was it that nothing ever passed by *Amai*? Naniso and Shinga glanced at each other nervously.

'I don't know what's going on here, but you might as well get ready for school. It's good to see you are feeling better Naniso,' *Amai* said firmly.

Naniso's face fell. There was no point trying to convince her mother otherwise. Much to Naniso's annoyance, her brother gave her a reassuring smile and a pat on her back. As *Amai* ushered them out of the cupboard, they didn't see a warm glow, golden just like the rays of the sun, fade away inside the *mbira*.

CHAPTER 5

BAO THE BAOBAB

Over in the savannah plains of *Tirivhu*, Bao, a mystical baobab tree stood with his branches hanging low. It was a sorrowful sight and not one to be expected of such a majestic and legendary being. He had an enormous trunk with a hollow entrance that led to many chambers inside. All species of animal took shelter inside Bao. It certainly made a perfect place to play hide and seek. When you looked closely at his bark, you could also see a magical pattern that shifted like changing lights. It certainly was a mystical tree.

Sitting beneath Bao, at her favorite little table was *Gogo* Zana. Here she was known as Zana because no one knew her age. She didn't know her age either. On the table was a teapot and two tea cups. Zana had a cheeky smile on her face as she hummed to herself and played an instrument.

It was a *mbira*.

She stroked the metal keys, a golden glow just like the rays of the sun flowed from the *mbira* into Bao's hollow entrance. Responding to the glow, Bao spoke.

'Kumhanya handi kusvika...'

'...Slow and steady wins the race,' Zana replied.

Bao sighed. 'Zana, if you understand what I mean, then why do you keep disturbing the twins in the mornings? Don't be too hasty. Things must follow their natural course.'

'Aah, it's not just for fun you know. *Vazukuru* need a little help. Natural course this and natural course that! It's all taking a bit too long don't you think? Hey, did you see they almost caught me today?' she chuckled, much to Bao's disapproval.

Zana understood very well why Bao was a little nervous. He needed help fast, so the plan could not fail. He was withering away and hadn't flowered fruit for years. In the meantime, her fingers were aching with blisters from years of constantly playing her *mbira*. The golden glow flowing from it was all that kept Bao from toppling over. It boosted Bao's own glow. She knew that if the glow inside him faded, he would die. The twins were the key to Bao's survival – they had to take over from Zana soon.

Suddenly a gust of wind twirled 'round and 'round Zana and Bao. It gathered the soil and dead leaves on the ground creating a mini tornado. The dust set Zana off into a coughing fit. Defying her unknown age, she swiftly stood up, grabbed her colourful walking stick and pointed it at the whirlwind in a defensive stance. She knew it was Nhema in one of his many disguises. The few birds perched on Bao's branches quickly flew away with fright and the small creatures in his hollow trunk remained hidden. The sky changed colour from blue to purple to grey.

Nhema was Zana's evil and cunning brother. Of course, Zana would never say that about him. He was her brother after all. A long time ago, he was a *muchengeti*, a guardian of the old treasures, but one who did not want the treasures shared with anyone. He was assigned to protect Bao. An unfortunate incident with the humans, which had prevented him from protecting Bao, led him to believe that the people of the new day were ungrateful, inconsiderate and disrespectful. He became bitter and angry and wanted nothing more to do with being a *muchengeti*. If the humans wanted chaos, he would give them more chaos than they could ever imagine. His mission now was to use tricks and lies to make the treasure's glow fade across the land.

'Well, well,' Nhema sneered, 'not doing too well are you Bao? Oh, why the sad face old man? Give up the glow! Those kids will never want to know you. They are way too busy wanting to be somebody else.'

'*Enda*! Be gone Nhema!' Zana shouted. 'There's nothing for you here!'

'Nothing yet *hanzvadzi*,' Nhema retorted with an evil laugh. 'Nothing yet.' Then he vanished.

The mini tornado disappeared just as quickly as it had appeared. The sky turned from grey to purple to blue again. A few small animals crept out of Bao's hollow trunk and scurried about. There was a calm silence between the two old friends.

'Don't lose hope my friend,' Bao tried to comfort Zana. 'I believe because of your antics there's been a spark. Naniso and Shinga will soon take their place as *vachengeti*,' Bao declared with new-found confidence.

'A spark?! You see it too?!' Zana could not hide her excitement. 'That means they are ready! Yes! Yes!' She clapped her hands in delight. 'Wonderful! Come on then! Lift your branches up. It might help them more if you stopped behaving as if you are already dead!' Zana teased Bao with a twinkle in her eye.

'*Iwe* Zana,' Bao scolded her lovingly before agreeing. 'Okay I will,' he huffed as he struggled to raise his branches.

As he did, the same golden glow, like the one that had flowed from the *mbira* flooded the sub-Saharan landscape. A shower of golden dust sprayed from his leaves. Zana was overcome with joy as she danced and leaped in the air. Her ululations echoed across the mountains far in the distance.

CHAPTER 6

THE PRESENTATION

Back in England, Naniso was dreading school. She just couldn't face the teasing from Rita and her minions. Thankfully, Miss Harrison, who was also their class teacher, came to the rescue in the first lesson when she announced a competition. Nothing created a frenzy of excitement like a competition.

'You must work in pairs. Pick an object, any object that you both agree on. You must then create a presentation explaining why you selected that object and what's special about it. All the classes are taking part and the best from each will go on to the finals. The winner will present at the parents' assembly.'

Miss Harrison seemed just as excited as her children. She paired the students up herself by picking names from a glass jar. When their friends Sanjay and Carmen were quickly paired off with other students, the twins were disappointed. As if things couldn't get worse they ended up being a pair! Both Naniso and Shinga protested.

'We live together, so we'll have an unfair advantage on the others!' Shinga argued.

'He's my brother! Can I work with someone else pleeease?' pleaded Naniso.

'I can only do what the jar tells me,' replied Miss Harrison after listening patiently. 'Now can we get on with our English lesson?'

After school, they went straight home, especially because it was...raining. As soon as they walked through the door, they wasted no time in collecting the items for their assignment.

They figured it was best to get it over and done with and within minutes, they laid out a violin, a football, a basketball and a half-eaten slice of pizza on the dining room table.

Naniso being the musical one had of course chosen the violin. She couldn't help but think that if she'd been paired with Carmen, who liked the same things as she did, they would have both chosen instruments and created an orchestra. What on earth would a violin have to do with balls and pizza? She glared at her brother willing him to explain himself as he took a big bite out of the pizza slice.

'What?' he asked defensively, though that didn't stop him from licking his lips. 'Miss Harrison said anything right?'

Naniso knew her brother was ready for an argument. He was good at debating and always had to have the last word. She let him continue.

'Actually, we can look at this football and basketball as instruments. You see they are instrumental to the game. Get it?!' he said with a wink.

'Why did you bring pizza?' Naniso demanded. 'Is that instrumental to your tummy?'

'That's right,' Shinga sniggered with his mouth full. 'Just so you know, I am not playing that violin.'

Naniso stuck her tongue out at him.

They stood staring at the items on the table. There was much discussion and arguing on which item to choose, but as they were both competitive, they knew that if they wanted to win, they had to work together.

'Well if we really want to be different, we should talk about something no one else would think of,' Naniso finally said. 'How about something from Zimbabwe?'

'I'm not sure. The audience might get bored. They won't get it. Everyone likes football, so we should definitely use the football at least,' said Shinga.

'Well, you could earn some brownie points from *Amai* and *Baba* after that stunt you pulled when you refused to say *makadi* to *Tete*.' Naniso was referring to the day when Shinga refused to respectfully greet *Tete*, their father's sister in their Shona language.

'I mean, how hard was it to just say three syllables. *Ma-ka-di*. That was all you had to say,' she laughed.

Shinga briefly considered the idea and agreed. If he got back in their good books on this matter, he could possibly persuade them to buy him a new video game. He zoomed out of the kitchen and returned with the box that contained *Amai's* cherished possessions. He almost tipped the contents out as he placed the box on the table.

'We don't know much about any of these things,' Naniso said, carefully lifting out the instruments one by one.

First, she took out the *mbira*, then the *vuvuzela*, then the *hosho* and finally the *ngoma*. The twins were immediately drawn towards the *mbira*. Naniso was instantly reminded of her encounter with *Gogo* Zana. It was weird how *Amai's mbira* looked like the one the old lady had.

As Shinga lifted the instrument to inspect it the most terrifying thing happened. The *mbira* slipped out of his clumsy hands and crashed on the cold, hard kitchen tiles.

The deafening sound of wood and metal colliding with stone left them frozen on the spot with their mouths wide open.

Naniso could only stare at the *calabash* as it spun noisily on the floor until it finally came to a stop. Looking at each other, wide-eyed, they waited for *Amai's* shout demanding an explanation for the ruckus. To their relief she was chatting to someone on the phone. Phew! Naniso slowly picked up the *mbira*.

'Sorry...,' Shinga sheepishly whispered with a grin.

Unimpressed Naniso kissed her teeth. 'Honestly, butter fingers! You are so annoying!'

Surprisingly, the *mbira* was neither broken nor damaged despite it being so old. Its keys were rusty, dusty and even housed a cobweb. It was definitely not as clean and sparkly as their mother liked things to be.

'This is it Shinga. If we do our presentation on this, we stand a good chance of winning.'

They discussed their options. It was obvious that at least half the class would turn up with football stuff and brag about their favorite teams. Now focused on getting a new video game, Shinga agreed with Naniso. Naniso on the other hand was desperate to win so that she could redeem herself from the croaking-toad incident.

'The *mbira* it is,' Shinga said, 'even though we don't know anything about it.'

'Let's google it,' Naniso suggested.

'How cool would it be if we could actually play it!' Shinga was now very excited.

'I can,' Naniso said casually.

Her brother looked at her doubtfully. He knew she was musical, but he'd never heard or seen her play anything other than her violin, piano or recorder. In the meantime, Naniso was getting comfortable and blowing the dust off the rusty keys. Cradling the sound board, she began plucking at the keys with her thumbs. Just as she had done in the park with *Gogo* Zana. Something was wrong though. The plucking produced an unpleasant, scratching noise – the noise that hurts your teeth!

'Please keep that noise down!' *Amai* shouted from the living room. 'I'm on the phone!'

'Oh, please Naniso stop it,' Shinga begged.

'But I can play. *Gogo* Zana...'

'You have never played a *mbira* in your life. You don't have to know everything you know.'

Shinga shook his head and went to the computer in the corner of the dining room. He typed '*mbira*' in Google and started his research.

Soon he discovered that of the many types of *mbira*, theirs was a *nyunganyunga*. He suggested that their presentation be about both the violin and *mbira*, meaning Naniso would get a chance to show off her violin-playing skills if playing the *mbira* didn't work out. As her brother doubted her ability, she became eager to prove him wrong. She had to see the old woman again. As bizarre as their first encounter was, she had to return to the park. She had to find *Gogo* Zana.

CHAPTER 7

BEAUTIFUL BIRD

Saturday was for football and dance but both clubs had been cancelled due to the wet and windy weather. As soon as there was a break in the rain, Naniso convinced her parents they had to go to the park for some fresh air. She packed *Amai's mbira* in her rucksack, slung it over her shoulder and led her family out of the front door.

It was a long shot but as soon as they arrived at the park, she headed for the oak tree hoping *Gogo* Zana would be there. Shinga followed her but she barely noticed him. There was no one except for a bird looking for some food. It was the same one that *Gogo* Zana had tried to shoo away the last time they were under the tree.

Naniso sat down and chased the bird away. Again, the best it could do was hop off. She pulled the *mbira* out of her bag. Unsure about what to do, she started to pluck at the keys. Miraculously, this time, her fingers did not fail her, and they created a soothing and beautiful rhythm. She found herself lost in its enchantment and closed her eyes as she had done with *Gogo* Zana. She soon realised that she was playing the same mysterious melody that had woken her and Shinga up at five o'clock every morning, all week. The music soon made her relax, and she felt as if she was flying, weaving through branches to the top of the tree, towards a golden sky. She was free and happy. Shinga was coming up right behind her in full superhero pose, just as Shinga would do. Suddenly, a shrill little voice brought her back to earth.

'Please move. You're sitting right on top of my worms. Can you move over please?'

Naniso controlled her urge to scream and reassured herself that there had to be a perfectly reasonable explanation as to why a bird, a beautiful one at that, was talking to her. What was it lately with her getting in people's way? First it was *Gogo* Zana's foot and now...a talking bird's lunch? She then noticed that she was sitting under a tree that was **not** an oak tree, but a big, fat one with a hole in the middle and long, heavy branches. The park was now a wide savannah land, like the one on *The Lion King*, and the cold, winter air was replaced by a warm breeze.

'I need to get to the worms. Do you mind moving over a bit please?' asked the bird politely.

She moved out of the bird's way. Its wings were long and wide, and its feathers were all the shades of purple.

'Whoa!' Naniso gasped.

Suddenly there was a gentle gust of wind as a bunch of leaves swirled in the air and, much to Naniso's surprise, started singing and dancing:

Shiri yakanaka unoendepi?
Huya uya titambe

63

Naniso decided to test this new-found line of communication, even though she was not expecting a response.

'Hi I'm Naniso. Where's your family?'

'I'm *Gondo Shiri* and my family is up there,' the bird replied as it lifted its left wing and pointed to the sky. Naniso stayed calm. What was the use in panicking at this point?

'Wow!' she gasped.

Looking up, she saw hundreds of birds flying in the sky. Their beautiful wings created colourful swirls of light, as they twittered and dived in and out of the sun's rays. She knelt next to *Gondo Shiri*. He looked out of place on the ground. He clearly didn't belong there.

'Why are you down here and not up there with the others?' she asked.

'I like it here. The leaves, the flowers...'

'He's a scaredy cat. In fact, maybe if a real cat chased him, he might take to the sky,' interrupted a chameleon that had been watching them from inside the tree trunk.

'You're not helping,' Naniso said to the chameleon. 'How about that?' she said to no one in particular. 'I can talk to animals.'

'I don't fly any further than the tree tops,' *Gondo Shiri* responded matter-of-factly. 'I have friends down here who like to play with me. They even sing a special song just for me. Listen.'

The fallen leaves immediately swirled up again and performed their song and dance routine, over and over and over:

Shiri yakanaka unoendepi?
Huya uya titambe

'Blah! Blah! Blah! The truth is *Gondo Shiri* broke his wing and his family had to wait for him to get better. Even though his wing is stronger now, he's afraid that if he flies above the treetops, he'll fall back down and disappoint his family. Those bad leaves and their song do not help at all!' The chameleon explained it all.

'Is this true?' asked Naniso, as she lifted the bird onto her knee.

'I guess,' *Gondo Shiri* replied shyly, at which the chameleon rolled her eyes.

'You're a bird. You're supposed to fly,' Naniso pointed out.

'I don't feel strong enough yet. It's safe for me here,' was *Gondo Shiri's* reply.

'But no one will see how beautiful you are if you stay down here. Your wing looks strong to me *Gondo Shiri*. Stop being afraid and try. Are you truly happy here? What about your family? They must miss you.'

The leaves started to swirl around them faster and faster and sang their song even louder and louder. They clearly did not like Naniso's line of thinking, so they urged *Gondo Shiri* to come along and play.

Shiri yakanaka unoendepi?
Huya uya titambe

This time, Naniso also started to sing. It was the song she'd been playing on the *mbira* and for the first time she remembered where she'd heard

67

it before. It was on holiday in Zimbabwe, when she was nine years old. *Mbuya* had taught them the song, and what fun they'd had learning to pronounce the words. They'd banged spoons on colourful enamel cups and plates for percussion and danced and laughed so hard until their insides hurt.

As she sang, she realised what was missing. *Gondo Shiri* and the fallen leaves kept repeating the same two lines over and over. The song was incomplete. As she listened, she watched them closely too and saw that the leaves were not playing nice. They created a mini tornado around *Gondo Shiri*, flinging dust in his eyes. They laughed when he lost his balance and tumbled to the ground. Naniso realised that the fallen leaves were not the bird's friends after all. They were trying to stop him from taking to the skies where he belonged.

The leaves were jealous of *Gondo Shiri's* beautiful wings. His wings reminded them of when they were once jewels on the tree, shining bright with dew drops in the sunlight. They were cunningly keeping *Gondo Shiri* grounded with them. It wasn't fair! They were keeping him from joining his family and most of all from being a bird. *Gondo Shiri* needed help and she had to do something fast, so she allowed herself to complete the song:

> *Ndiri kuenda kumakore*
> *Kuti ndifanane nemakore*

'*Gondo Shiri*, sing along with me!' Naniso shouted.

The fallen leaves danced frantically and sang louder, trying to drown out Naniso's voice. The mini tornado became a medium-sized tornado with Naniso right in the middle of it. The chameleon, who was still watching everything, started to sing with Naniso. Scurrying up and down the tree and across the branches, she sang at the top of her voice encouraging the flowers and the leaves on the trees and the other birds to sing along with Naniso. Soon the atmosphere was filled with a harmonious melody:

Shiri yakanaka unoendepi?
Huya uya titambe
Ndiri kuenda kumakore
Kuti ndifanane nemakore

Then suddenly, the leaves quietened down, and the medium-sized tornado became a mini tornado then a whirlwind then a breeze, then the air stood still. *Gondo Shiri* had taken off and was soaring up the baobab tree. The chameleon and Naniso cheered him on until he made it past the tree tops. There was a loud cheer. He'd done it!

'This is awesome!' *Gondo Shir*i called out. 'Look what I can do!' He did a few somersaults in the air. 'Thank you Naniso!'

'Goodbye!' she called back to him.

Naniso, the chameleon and the fallen leaves watched as *Gondo Shiri* and his family flew away. He was free to be the bird he was born to be.

'Good job *muchengeti*. I guess this is now farewell until next time.'

'My name is Naniso in fact,' she corrected her.

'Yes, yes indeed that is your name. Farewell,' the chameleon nodded and turned to go.

'I don't understand...,' Naniso began.

The chameleon sighed and turned back. 'This has Zana written all over it. You are after all talking to a chameleon my child.'

Zana? The old woman in the park? Naniso smiled to herself. She'd known it. There was something strange about that woman.

'You need to learn these things yourself young lady. There is only so much we can do,' tutted the chameleon.

Naniso was confused. 'A little help here please?'

The chameleon sighed. 'What did you just teach *Gondo Shiri*?'

'Not to be afraid and do what he was made to do. To be brave and fly up to the clouds and be proud of who he is. Oh! It's a lesson for me too?!'

'My work here is done. Now it's time for you to fly,' the chameleon smiled as she nodded towards the *mbira*. "You play very well *muchengeti*. Protector of our legacy. I, *Rwaivi* the chameleon, am always at your service.'

Naniso picked up the *mbira*.

'Is this a magical *mbira*?" she asked.

Rwaivi had already slipped away into the hole in the tree trunk. Naniso looked at the hole and thought she could make out a face. Not thinking much of it she sat down with the *mbira* on her lap. Her thumbs and index finger danced over the keys playing the mysterious melody.

As though waking up from a deep sleep, she was back in the park sitting under the oak tree. The bird had gone and Shinga was carefully climbing down the tree.

'What are you doing Shinga?'

'I told you I was going to climb that tree seeing that none of my friends were here to play with me,' replied Shinga.

'Huh?'

'Honestly, Naniso, I swear you live on another planet sometimes. Anyway, climbing that tree was awesome! This is going to sound weird right, but I'm sure I was flying up in the clouds, and... oh you wouldn't get it anyway. C'mon let's go on the swings!'

'I do get it,' Naniso responded, but Shinga was already on his way across the park to the swings.

CHAPTER 8

BAO STRENGTHENS

It was presentation day.

Helping Miss Harrison judge the competition were Mr Waterhead, the Headmaster and Mrs Moore, the Year 4 teacher. First up, Takao and Mason invited the class to join in a Japanese tea-making ritual complete with costume. Then Nia performed a tap dance but Rita who was her partner sat sulking at her desk. This pairing had obviously not worked. There were then lots and lots of presentations about football and favourite

Premier League teams. Then it was Naniso and Shinga's turn.

'*Pamwe*!' They high-fived each other.

Shinga started by naming some of the national instruments from around the world before talking about the *mbira*.

'England has the concertina, Finland the violin and Brazil the guitar. The *mbira* is Zimbabwe's national instrument. It's usually accompanied by singing, drums called *ngoma* and rattles called *hosho*. This is a *nyunganyunga mbira* which originates from Mozambique and is played in worship, at weddings and funerals too. Being a national instrument, it's taught in schools.'

Naniso then described the *mbira*.

'...here's the wooden calabash resonator called *deze*. It makes the sound louder. The soundboard called *gwariva* nests the fifteen metal keys. When you play the keys these bottle tops make a percussion sound just like a waterfall. The *mbira* can be heard in traditional and modern music played by some of Zimbabwe's famous artists. People around the world are learning to play it too.'

Presentation Day!

'Now here's the violin. The violin, although from a different part of the world, makes a perfect musical partner for the *mbira*.'

Shinga was about to signal Miss Harrison to play a YouTube video of musicians playing both instruments when Naniso started plucking at the *mbira* keys. He adjusted his glasses and nervously started tapping his fingers on his thigh.

'Oh no! What is she doing?' he mumbled to himself. 'This is going to be a disaster!'

Then he heard his sister playing the mysterious melody but better than it sounded at five o'clock. She was playing brilliantly! His sister sure was full of surprises. How had she learned to play in such a short time? Watching her fingers dart across the keys in a steady rhythm, he could have sworn he saw a golden glow inside the *calabash*.

Captivated by the music, one by one the twins' classmates left their seats and stood around Naniso to watch her play. They all wanted to have a go at this new-found instrument. All except Rita. She stayed glued to her chair, glaring at everyone.

Naniso started to sing along and Shinga and their classmates joined in, dancing and clapping:

Shiri yakanaka unoendepi
Huya uya titambe
Ndiri kuenda kumakore
Kuti ndifanane nemakore

Miss Harrison was delighted the twins had managed to work well together. Naniso, who was all smiles, knew that she could sing the solo at the parents' assembly. In the end though, it was Takao and Mason who were chosen to represent their class at the finals.

As Naniso played the *mbira, Gogo* Zana was merrily dancing beneath the graceful branches of majestic Bao, the baobab tree. With the twins sharing the story of the *mbira* with others, Bao was becoming stronger and stronger. All the animals took shelter from the hot sun under his shade. Birds perched on his branches, tweeting joyfully. *Tsuro* were bouncing in and out of his trunk.

A mummy baboon watched her seven children swing from branch to branch. It was a happy scene until a sudden chill filled the air and a dark cloud moved slowly across the landscape.

'I wouldn't be celebrating if I were you.' It was Nhema, sneering at Bao. 'You just have the girl's interest, but the boy is not ready. I will make sure he will never be ready! A little song is not going to save you Bao.'

Gogo Zana looked directly at her brother and rebuked him. 'Tsk! What is wrong with you? Leave that boy alone. He has the same right just like you had to share in the wealth of his inheritance! The legacy will never give up. A song might seem trivial to you Nhema but know there is always a reward in trying all things.'

And of course, Bao being Bao, he just had to confirm these words with a *tsumo*:

'Chenga ose manhanga hapana risina mhodzi.'

Glossary

Amai	mother
Baba	father
Enda	go
Famba zvakanaka	walk properly
Gogo	grandmother
Gondo	eagle
Hanzvadzi	sister (*if a brother is speaking*), brother (*if a sister is speaking*)
Hosho	rattle, musical instrument that usually accompanies a drum
Iwe	you
Kurumidza	hurry up
Makadi	how are you
Mbira	thumb piano
Mbuya	grandmother
Muchengeti	guardian

Muzukuru	grandchild
Ngoma	drum
Nhema	untruth
Nyunganyunga	type of thumb piano, also called kalimba
Pamwe	together
Rwaivi	chameleon
Sekuru	grandfather
Shiri	bird
Tete	paternal aunt
Tirivhu	we are earth
Tsumo	proverb
Tsuro	hare
Vachengeti	guardians
Vazukuru	grandchildren
Vuvuzela	a long musical horn commonly used at football matches in South Africa
Zana	hundred

Kumhanya handi kusvika – running does not mean you will get there. This is a proverb/saying meaning 'do not rush'.

Chenga ose manhanga hapana risina mhodzi – take care of all the pumpkins, there is none without seed. This is a proverb that means we should treat everyone equally because we are all important.

Shiri Yakanaka — this is a song that children in Zimbabwe sing and dance to during play. It is also often used as a lullaby. You can listen to a version of it at *www.nanisocreate.com*

Shona lyrics:
Shiri yakanaka
Unoendepi?
Huya uya titambe
Ndiri kuenda kumakore
Kuti ndifanane nemakore

English Translation:
Beautiful bird
Where are you going?
Come and play with me
I am going to the clouds
So I can be just like the clouds

ABOUT THE AUTHOR

SP K-Mushambi is happiest when she is creating. It could be writing a song, baking a yummy cake or inventing her own version of the latest dance craze (which according to reliable sources means she is doing it all wrong). She enjoys getting to know different cultures and how they are related to her own heritage.

Born in England and raised in Zimbabwe, she has had a career in banking and corporate treasury which spans over twenty years. She lives in Berkshire with her husband and their two daughters.

About Naniso Create

Naniso Create is the home of Naniso Media, a young start-up with a big vision, birthed from the founders' experience of growing up in Zimbabwe and raising children in the UK.

Naniso Media is guided by the motto 'Imagine it. Create it. Inspire.' Their objective is to use storytelling, education and events in a fun and imaginative way to bring children closer to the rich cultural and historical heritage of Zimbabwe, wherever they may be in the world.

To find out more about the twins and their friends go to: *www.nanisoshinga.com.*

Imagine it. Create it. Inspire...

CPSIA information can be obtained
at www.ICGtesting.com
Printed in the USA
LVHW072306240620
658908LV00029B/1513

9 781916 121706